THE YETIS HUNT
FOR SIR QUINTON!
D0865826
520 282 77 5

CATNIP BOOKS
Published by Catnip Publishing Ltd.
14 Greville Street
London EC1N 8SB

This edition published 2009
1 3 5 7 9 10 8 6 4 2

A CIP catalogue record of this book is available from the British Library

ISBN 978-1-846470-70-7

Printed in Poland

THE YETIS HUNT FOR SIR QUINTON!

Illustrated by
Judy Brown

CHAPTER ONE

In which Sir Quinton loses his temper and confronts his rival

Hello there! I am Sir Quinton Quest, the world famous explorer, and I am **furious**! Furious, indignant, and jolly well hopping mad! I'll tell you why.

The other night, I decided to call into the Explorer's Club. I fancied a relaxing evening away from Quest Towers. My good wife, Lady Cynthia, was on the telephone gossiping with her cronies and Muggins, my butler, was spring cleaning.

I spend a lot of time at the Club, where they do a good Explorer Club Sandwich.

I have my own chair there. It's warm and comfortable and usually peaceful, so I can concentrate on the crossword in the *Daily Explorer*.

ACROSS
3. WHAT EXPLORERS HOPE BRIDGES WON'T DO... ALSO A FAVOURITE EXPLORER PUDDING
4. ONE WHO MAKES EXPLORERS' TEA.

DOWN
1. EXPLORERS GO EXPLORING HERE
2. WHAT EXPLORERS DO ON MOUNTAINS.

I strolled into the lounge and got the shock of my life!

Let me explain something here. Hanging in pride of place in the lounge, above the mantelpiece, is a large, framed photograph of my good self. It was taken last year, on my triumphant return from the Himalayas. In it, I am holding the coveted Explorer Of The Year Challenge Cup. I have won this splendid Cup for a record six years running – and rightfully so. I am proud of the photograph, and think my moustache has come out particularly well.

Muggins asked if he could be in it, but I said no. Granted he was with me on the expedition, but only because I needed him to pull the sledge and wash up.

So what did I see? **My photo!**

vandalized!

I couldn't believe my eyes!

Many of my fellow explorers have cause to envy me, of course. But this was beyond the pale. Who had done such a dastardly thing?

I knew. Oh, I knew all right. It was that young upstart, Ffoothold.

Findley Ffoothold. Him with the ridiculous hair and the over-priced climbing boots and a tooth that goes "**ting**". We have a dark history, Ffoothold and I. He considers himself my rival. His cheek knows no bounds. Once, I even caught him sitting in **MY CHAIR**, can you believe!

He's young, ambitious, and always getting his picture in the paper, I can't think why.

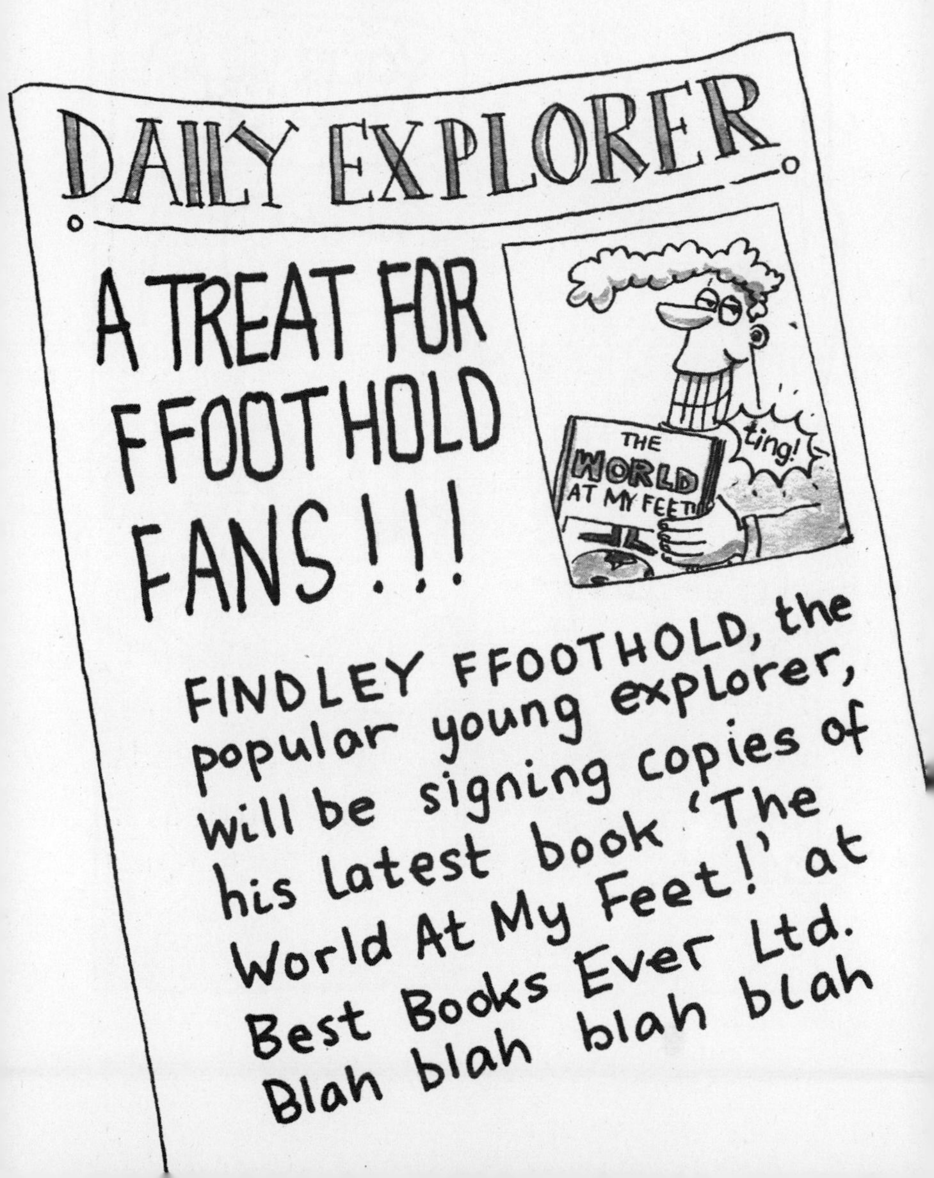

DAILY EXPLORER

A TREAT FOR FFOOTHOLD FANS!!!

FINDLEY FFOOTHOLD, the popular young explorer, will be signing copies of his latest book 'The World At My Feet!' at Best Books Ever Ltd. Blah blah blah blah

I confronted him, of course. I don't take insults like this lying down.

He denied all knowledge, but I knew it was him. Pure jealousy, of course. Just because he's never won the Cup.

I stormed out, taking the photograph with me. I would get Muggins to see what he could do.

Muggins is very loyal. He would be as shocked as I was at this act of carnage.

CHAPTER TWO

In which Sir Quinton
recounts his
last expedition

Now will be a good time to tell you a little more about my famed expedition which led to me yet again winning the Challenge Cup.

To be honest, the main reason for the expedition was to put Ffoothold in his place. The young pup was actually claiming to have found evidence for the existence of the Yeti, a creature of myth, otherwise known as the Abominable Snowman. It was all over the newspapers. A blurry photograph of what he insisted was a genuine Yeti footprint.

Ridiculous! Everyone knows that Yetis are made up. I was determined to prove him wrong, with his wild claims and ludicrous hair. Muggins and I immediately set off on a trip to the Himalayas.

Lady Cynthia remained behind and had a quiet time, as always.

The Himalayas were **freezing**. I had a hard time of it. Oh, the sufferings I endured! A lesser man would have given up.

Alone, we travelled the frozen wastes. No sign of any Yetis.

We camped in sub-zero temperatures.
Not a Yeti in sight.

That night, wolves got into our supply tent and made off with our food. Well, we think it was wolves. It could have been bears.

The next day, I accidentally fell over a precipice. Luckily, my foot caught in a small branch or something and I landed unhurt on a ledge below.

Unfortunately I got lost and was forced to use the Yeti horn – a non-sensical contraption given to me as a birthday present by Lady Cynthia.

She ordered it from the Explorer's Catalogue, which I'm afraid to say features a lot of useless tat. It was supposed to make the sound of a Yeti love call. Love call? More like a constipated hippopotamus.

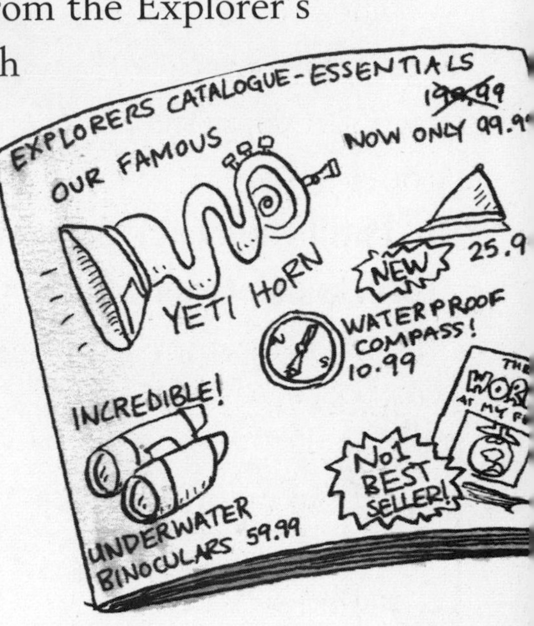

I still maintain the resulting avalanche was a coincidence.

I can't really remember much after that. I must had some sort of white out. I don't know how I made it back to base camp, but I did. Having lost most of our equipment, we were forced to abandon the quest and catch the next plane home. Not that it mattered. I saw no Yetis.

Well, Muggins claimed that **he** had, but he was suffering from snow madness so I ignored him.

And there you have it. I presented the **SOCIETY OF FAMOUS EXPLORERS** (**SOFE**) with my many photographs of plain, mint condition snow with no sign of any footprints, was awarded the Cup and got my photograph displayed in the lounge.

Ffoothold didn't like it, of course. You should have seen his face.

CHAPTER THREE

In which Sir Quinton returns to Quest Towers

Anyway, back to the present. I was in a poor mood when I returned to Quest Towers and told Lady Cynthia and Muggins about the outrage.

Sometimes Lady Cynthia can be less than supportive. It didn't help when she informed me that she was thinking of holding one of her jam and knitting parties, when a load of dreary women take over the place. I would make sure to be out **that** evening, I can tell you.

Muggins said he would see what he could do to repair the damage to the photograph. I retired to my study and dashed off a strong letter of complaint to the ***Daily Explorer***.

Sirs,

I am writing to complain in the strongest possible terms about the photograph of myself which hangs in the Explorer's Club. To my horror, I find that it has been tampered with. I name no names, but suspect a certain young upstart (initials F Ff) who bears me a grudge. He has no business being in SOFE and I strongly suggest he is thrown out.

Yours furiously

Sir Quinton Quest

(Explorer of the Year six times running.)

I went out, posted it, came home, went to bed and sulked.

CHAPTER FOUR

Meanwhile, in the Himalayas...

Hi there! Me think it time me introduce myself.
Me speakin' in Yeti language so need translation.
Real name is Squiggle Pine Tree
Wiggly Line, but you can call me Bob.

Last year, funny thing happen. Me see big iron bird come from sky, bringin' coupla weirdos.

Little fat bossy one and tall thin one who do all work. This very excitin'!

Me spy on weirdos. It fun! Me wear weirdos' clothes. Me think me look dead good. Me go show relations.

That night, me and relations pinch weirdos' grub, take back to cave, have big feast. It taste **GOOD**, yum yum!

Next day, little fat weirdo go off walkin'. We follow.

Him get in lotta trouble. We help. We good like that.

Him got funny horn, make big noise. Him blow, make big avalanche. Him buried.

We dig him up. Him frozen solid. Very slippery. We push him off down mountain. Quickest way. Tall thin weirdo thaw him out.

Then big iron bird come and take them away.

We Yetis dead sad when weirdos go. We miss them. Specially little fat one, him big laugh.

We go back to secret cave. Nothin' to do now. Not feel like singin', not feel like makin' jokes. No grub. We bored again.

We make shrine. Make big display all things little fat weirdo leave behind. Best of all is big horn. We find under snow. We not blow it. Got too much respect. Besides, we not stupid, it make big avalanche.

We look at shrine one whole year. We hope him come back, but no.

One day me sittin' lookin' sadly at shrine and me notice somethin'. Little brass plate screwed on horn. It say weirdo words.

Me get Yeti-Weirdo dictionary, look up words.

Hey! Result! We know weirdo's name and where him live!

We very excited. We have big talk. We make plan!

Plan is, **WE TAKE HOLIDAY**. We go on big iron bird, see bit of London, England, go to little fat weirdo's house, give him lovely surprise and give back lost horn.

You see? I tell you we kind hearted. See you later!

CHAPTER FIVE

In which Sir Quinton re-hangs his photograph, has breakfast and adds to his hate list.

The following morning, I asked Muggins how he was getting on with cleaning up my defaced photgraph. He said he had done what he could.

Frankly, I was disappointed with his efforts.

Never the less, I was determined that the photograph should go back in its rightful place immediately, so I set off for the Club.

Who should be there, lounging around as usual, but Ffoothold. I marched past him and hung the photograph back on it's hook.

"There!" I said, loudly. "That's better."

Then I stood back and gave him a meaningful glare. He smirked, which annoyed me highly.

"Looking a bit worse for wear, isn't it, pops? he observed.

"When **you** win the Challenge Cup six years running, I might be interested in your opinion," I said, coldly. "But not before."

"Yeah, well," he drawled. "Time it got replaced if you ask me. Need a bit of young blood round here."

I wasn't going to stick around in the same room as the impertinent lout. Furiously, I marched out.

I wasn't sure where to go next. I didn't want to go home. Lady Cynthia was preparing for her jam and knitting evening and Muggins was helping her pick gooseberries and sharpen needles and wind wool and whatever it is she does on these occasions. I had told her I

wouldn't be home until after midnight.

I decided to go and have a full breakfast at **GREASY GEORGE'S**, the café across the road. They do a very good fry up.

I would while away a few hours reading the **Daily Explorer**. See if my letter of complaint had been published. If not, I would write a letter complaining about it.

There was nothing of interest in the paper and no sign of my letter. This put me in an even worse mood.

While I waited for my food, I decided to update my hate list. I keep a list of things that annoy me. I write them down in a book, which I carry with me everywhere. Everyone should have one.

Things that annoy me.

Findley Ffoothold
Findley Ffoothold's hair
Findley Ffoothold's boots
Findley Ffoothold's book
Green jam with seeds in
Home knitted trousers
Youth today
Bongo players
The skin on rice pudding
Papers that do not publish complaining letters.

My breakfast arrived and I was just about to tuck in when something caught my eye. That young bounder Ffoothold was sneaking out of the Club – and under his arm was a thin, square package wrapped in plain brown paper.

I raced from the café. I wasn't about to let him get away with this! Not content with defacing my photograph, he was actually **stealing** it! In broad daylight too! Clearly his evil intention was to dump it in a dustbin somewhere!

I caught him up just as he rounded the corner, and confronted him.

Despite my indignant demands, he refused to hand it over. I wasn't about to wrestle him to the ground. I like to maintain my dignity. I don't stoop to fighting in the street. Besides, he's bigger than me.

Fuming, I watched him stroll away.

There was only one thing I could do. Well, two things. I could report him to the police. But by the time they came to arrest him, he would most probably have disposed of the evidence. That left the one thing.

I followed him.

CHAPTER SIX

In which Bob and his relations take a trip

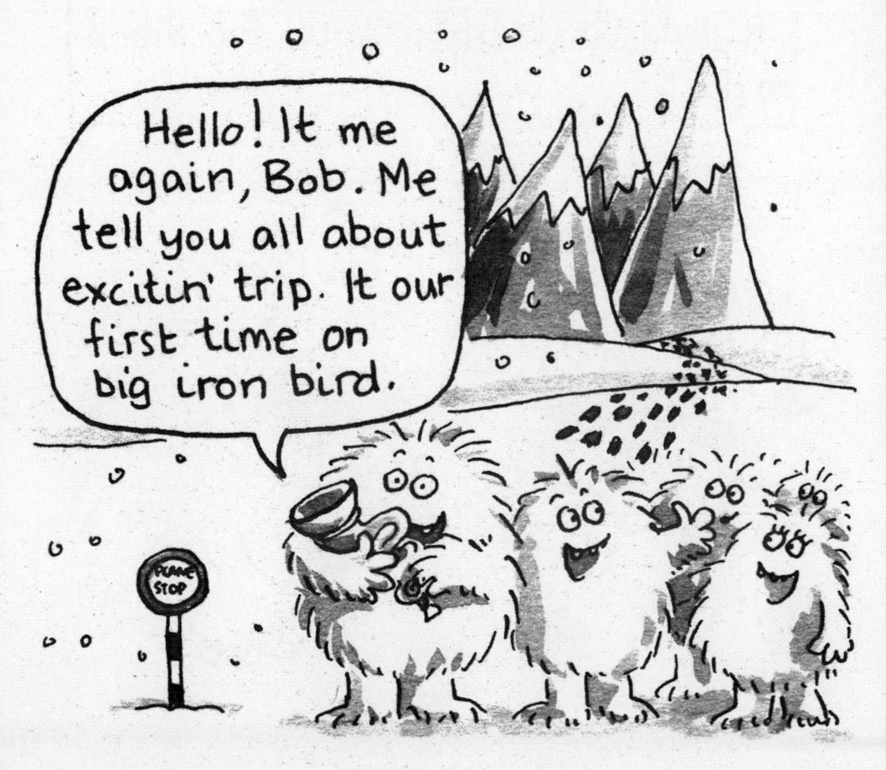

It dead good in bird. Lotta fun things to do.

We eat weirdo grub.

We try weirdo drink.

We watch in-flight movie. We cry at end when nanny go.

After long time, bird go down. Door open. We get out. Hooray, we in London, England.

Lotta weirdos everywhere. Lotta pointin' an' shoutin'. Me think we stick out a bit. Got to do somethin' to blend in.

Need disguise.

Disguise sorted. See you later!

CHAPTER SEVEN

In which Sir Quinton stalks Findley Ffoothold, using his explorer skills.

If there is one thing I excel at, it is stalking. The trick is to keep one's quarry within sight whilst not getting too close. Blending in with one's environment is an essential skill for a world-famous explorer like me.

I learnt it in the jungles of Borneo, on one of my many expeditions.

Ducking behind lampposts and pillar boxes, I followed Ffoothold, who seemed in no particular hurry.

First, he entered a book shop, where he brazenly moved his own silly book into a prominent position in the window. Has he no shame?

He came out and moved on, frequently pausing to admire himself in shop windows.

Then he got his hair curled and his nails polished. Is there no end to his vanity?

He was in there for some considerable time. Finally he emerged, still holding my photograph.

I was a little surprised that the scoundrel hadn't disposed of it by now.

What did he intend to do with it, I wondered?

He moved on – and I followed.

CHAPTER EIGHT

In which the Yetis catch the tourist bus

Me take photo of relations with red weirdos in dresses. They called Bee Feeters. Me look at feet, but they not bee feet, they normal.

We go on big slow wheel. It bit cramped.

We go to big house called Palace. We meet nice lady with spiky hat. We see bridge that keep breaking. Me don't know why.

No more time for sight seein'. It gettin' late. We make driver take us to little fat weirdo's place. We lookin' forward to seein' him. Big reunion comin' up! We not only ones come to see little fat weirdo. Him gotta lotta visitors.

We go in. See you later!

CHAPTER NINE

In which Sir Quinton bursts into Findley Ffoothold's bachelor pad

I can't say I enjoyed trailing Ffoothold. I watched him dawdle over coffees and get his boots cleaned, pausing occasionally to pose for photographs with deluded fans. Night was falling when he finally decided to call it a day and go home. Quite frankly, I was exhausted. Hours of stalking had taken it out of me. But I was determined to see it through.

I watched through the windows of his apartment block to see what the rascal would do.

I watched him enter the lift – then boldly made my move.

Evening, Perkins.
Hey! Where's Your visitor's pass?

You look lovely tonight, Sonia.
RECEPTION
Excuse me?

I marched in and made for the lift.

Up I went, to floor seven.

I immediately spotted Ffoothold's apartment. I applied my eye to the keyhole.

There stood the bounder with **my photograph** in his hands, smirking. Caught red handed! This was too much to bear. I could control myself no longer.

He looked alarmed to see me, as well he might. I strode into the room.

"Show me that photograph!" I demanded.

"Why?" he said.

"Because you stole it from the Club."

"No I didn't," he said.

"Yes you did. You defaced it, then stole it. Show it to me **now!**"

"Okay, okay, keep your hair on," he said. And turned it around to face me. . .

Oh.

CHAPTER TEN

In which the Yetis enjoy the party

Well! Talk about good time. That some party, me tell you.

Me and relations never seen nothin' like it. We eat, we drink, we laugh, we dance! No sign of little fat weirdo, but that not stop us from havin' good time.

We win prize for best costume, whatever that mean.

We sing Yeti songs. Me recite Yeti poetry.

We life and soul of party.

CHAPTER ELEVEN

In which Sir Quinton goes home, feeling silly.

Alone, I walked the empty streets. I confess I was feeling rather foolish.

I had wrongly accused Ffoothold of theft. He wouldn't forget that in a hurry. Of course, I was gracious enough to apologize, after he threatened to knock my block off. I even purchased a signed copy of his wretched book.

I didn't feel myself at all. Quite frankly, I just wanted to get home, go to bed and forget the whole sorry episode.

It was nearly midnight when I arrived home. At least Lady Cynthia's jam and knitting evening would be over. I wouldn't have to talk to anybody.

I pushed open the gates.

Walking up the drive seemed to take forever.

I was almost on my knees when I reached the front door.

Good time at the club, Quinny?
All right. How was your evening?
Oh you know, dear, quiet.

I was never more glad to be home. I decided not to mention the business with the photograph. Right now, all I wanted to do was retire to bed.

CHAPTER TWELVE

In which Bob and his relations go home

Well. This sad bit. We goin' home. We have great time in London, England, but fact is, we miss snow. Snow big thing for Yetis.

On big bird we buy smelly drinks from trolley. Not taste good.

All way home, we talk 'bout holiday. We sad we not see little fat weirdo at party. Me can't remember what me did with Yeti horn. Me hope him find it.

Hooray! We back in Himalayas!

Plenty snow! Go home to cave.

We make cave look good. Soon we throw big comin' home party, invite Yeti friends, tell them all 'bout adventures. Bet they dead jealous.

So. That 'bout it from me. Nice talkin' to you. Bye for now!

CHAPTER THIRTEEN

In which Sir Quinton discovers the Yeti horn and has a word with Muggins.

The following morning I arose and went down to breakfast. I was about to sit down when I noticed something very strange indeed.

What should I see lying in the corner but the Yeti horn! The horn that I assumed had been buried under the avalanche on my last, fateful expedition. How very peculiar!

I followed Muggins into the kitchen. Maybe he could shed some light.

Most mysterious. Almost as big a mystery as who was to blame for defacing my photograph. Ffoothold had denied all knowledge and after the embarrassment of the previous evening I was inclined to believe him.

It rather seemed that I would never know the identity of the culprit.

Oh well. Perhaps it was time to forget about it. I had made a bit of a fool of myself with young Ffoothold. I can't say I cared for the chap, but possibly I had misjudged him. I would let bygones be bygones. Never let it be said that I am the sort to bear a grudge. Besides, he's always at the Club. I couldn't stay away forever.

I decided then and there to take the bull by the horns. I would go to the Club and shake his hand, man to man.

I was unprepared for the scene that met my eyes!

That young whippersnapper Ffoothold had actually replaced my photograph with his own!

I was furious! Furious, indignant, and jolly well hopping mad!

I protested, of course, but nobody was on my side.

Disgusted, I marched out. I would go home and write another strong letter of protest.

On the way home, I saw a ridiculous headline. **YETIS SPOTTED IN LONDON!** I don't know. The Explorer goes from bad to worse and I intend to cancel my subscription.